MW00962179

LET YOUR INNER GOLDEN SPARKLE

SHINE

LET YOUR INNER GOLDEN SPARKLE

SHINE

THE LITTLE GIRL WHO NEVER STOPPED BELIEVING IN HERSELF

WRITTEN BY SARAH VIE

ILLUSTRATED BY JULIANA BRYKOVA

gatekeeper press™
Columbus, Ohio

Let Your Inner Golden Sparkle Shine: The Little Girl Who Never Stopped Believing in Herself

Published by Gatekeeper Press
2167 Stringtown Rd, Suite 109
Columbus, OH 43123-2989
www.GatekeeperPress.com

Copyright © 2020 by Sarah Van Der Steur
All rights reserved. Neither this book, nor any parts within it may be sold or reproduced in any form or by any electronic or mechanical means, including information storage and retrieval systems without permission in writing from the author. The only exception is by a reviewer, who may quote short excerpts in a review.

ISBN (hardcover): 9781642379822

Co-written with my Inner Child, who never felt seen and heard, this book is dedicated to all my little readers out there. My wish is that you discover your Golden Light and keep shining always.

Also dedicated to my four children, my granddaughter, and the future generations to come.

Can you see the Inner Sparkle within YOU?

Hey, beautiful little YOU . . .
Yes, that's right . . . YOU . . .
I have something magical that I wanted to share . . .
Something that I know to be TRUE . . .
Something that I learned and I want you to know too .
. .
Are you ready to feel it?
Are YOU ready?
Okay . . .
Turn the page and I'll tell YOU . . .

YOU have something very special inside of you . .
I call it Your Inner Golden Sparkle.
And it's within YOU . . .
In your body, and in everything you DO . . .
No matter what . . .
No matter how you feel . . .
No matter what you do . . .
Your Inner Sparkle is within YOU . . .

Remember . . .
It's there and this is what you do . . .
To connect and to find it within YOU . . .

Gently close your eyes . . .
Take a deep breath . . .
Cross your arms across your chest . . .

Notice the magic beating of your heart . . .
Thump thump thump thump . . .

Do you feel your heartbeat?
That is YOU!
That is Your Inner Golden Sparkle . . .
Now I'll show you when you can believe in YOU . . .

When you want to be included, but your
Friends leave you out . . .

Remember . . .
Gently close your eyes . . .
Take a deep breath . . .
Cross your arms across your chest . . .

Notice the magic beating of your heart . . .
Thump thump thump thump . . .
Do you feel your heartbeat?
That is YOU!

Feel Your Inner Golden Sparkle Shine . . .

When your teacher says your work is just not right . . .

Remember . . .
Gently close your eyes . . .
Take a deep breath . . .
Cross your arms across your chest . . .

Notice the magic beating of your heart . . .
Thump thump thump thump . . .
Do you feel your heartbeat?
That is YOU!
Feel Your Inner Golden Sparkle Shine . . .

When you are told that being 2nd
place is just not good enough . . .

Remember . . .
Gently close your eyes . . .
Take a deep breath . . .
Cross your arms across your chest . . .

Notice the magic beating of your heart . . .
Thump thump thump thump . . .
Do you feel your heartbeat?
That is YOU!
Feel Your Inner Golden Sparkle Shine . . .

When the lights turn off at the
end of the day and you are
feeling quite afraid . . .

Remember . . .
Gently close your eyes . . .
Take a deep breath . . .
Cross your arms across your chest . . .

Notice the magic beating of your heart . . .
Thump thump thump thump . . .
Do you feel your heartbeat?
That is YOU!
Feel Your Inner Golden Sparkle Shine . . .

When you feel like everyone
is watching, and you're afraid
you are not good enough . . .

Remember . . .
Gently close your eyes . . .
Take a deep breath . . .
Cross your arms across your chest . . .

Notice the magic beating of your heart . . .
Thump thump thump thump . . .
Do you feel your heartbeat?
That is YOU!
Feel Your Inner Golden Sparkle Shine . . .

When the skies turn dark and the thunder is too loud . . .

Remember . . .
Gently close your eyes . . .
Take a deep breath . . .
Cross your arms across your chest . . .

Notice the magic beating of your heart . . .
Thump thump thump thump . . .
Do you feel your heartbeat?
That is YOU!
Feel Your Inner Golden Sparkle Shine . . .

When you have to walk in alone on the first day of something new . . .

Remember . . .
Gently close your eyes . . .
Take a deep breath . . .
Cross your arms across your chest . . .

Notice the magic beating of your heart . . .
Thump thump thump thump . . .
Do you feel your heartbeat?
That is YOU!
Feel Your Inner Golden Sparkle Shine . . .

When you have to welcome that
new baby into your house . . .

Whatever you do . . .
Wherever you go . . .
Your Inner Golden Sparkle is
always ready to shine.

And when you feel the Sparkle within YOU . . .
YOU show others how to Sparkle TOO!

This book was written by Me, Sarah Vie, along with my inner golden child. Now all grown up, I help people at every age connect with their sparkle and shine!

Every person is rooted in love, and when we tune into the songs of our heart, we won't ever forget who we truly are.

Never stop believing in yourself and always share your authentic self with the world!

CPSIA information can be obtained
at www.ICGtesting.com
Printed in the USA
BVHW062029271220
596489BV00001B/1

9 781642 379822